Did you know

dog is God

spelled backwards?

Text copyright © 2008 Teri Bennett
Illustrations copyright © 2008 Teri Bennett/Lisa Wandrei.

Book and jacket design/layout by Lisa Wandrei.

First U.S. edition 2008

Library of Congress Cataloging-in-Publishing Data

Bennett, Teri

Angel Dog Austin: Did you know dog is God spelled backwards?

ISBN 0-9765322-2-0 (hardcover edition)
(Soft cover edition ISBN 0-9765322-3-9)

[Fiction]

This book was typeset in Chauncy and
American Typewriter.

The illustrations were done with pencil, watercolor,
digital illustration media, and photographic images.

Published by Teri Bennett/Simply different
www.simplydifferent.net

Printed in Canada.

In dedication
to God, who helps me
find Him in all things.
Teri

Special Thanks To:

My handsome, successful, dedicated husband and my wise, strong, talented sons. I thank God every day for binding us together. My parents, who not only taught, but lived the love of Jesus Christ. And to my extended family and friends, who live the truth of loving your family and neighbors as yourself. You are in my heart forever.

And to my dogs, both past and present, for representing God's love so well.

A heartfelt thanks and appreciation to my editors: Audrey, Jack, Karen, Mary, Anne, Betty, Shelly, Barb, Bonnie, Bernie, Bob, Pastor Dave, Kathy, John, Danna, Rick, Regina, Lori, Marla, Michelle, Denise, Terri, Keith, Tom, Stephanie, Kristina and all the Spiritual Hotline gals.

A special group hug to Lisa, our art director, for always being so easy to work with and for sharing her enormous talent with this book. The dogs and I love you.

– T.B. –

For Keith, DJ, Eleanor, Francesca and Allie (*aka* "Peanut") for inspiring the puppy in me.

For my angel dad and fellow dog lover, Joe, who, I am certain, spends most of his time in doggy heaven; angel son, Teddy, who taught me how fragile life really is; and angel dogs Gary and Barkley for their unconditional love.

Thanks Lisa T. for your mentorship, friendship, honesty and encouragement.
I wouldn't be where I am today without you.

And thank you Teri for the opportunity to collaborate on this book. It's been an adventure!

Did you know dog is God spelled backwards?

Story by Teri Bennett

Illustrations by Teri Bennett & Lisa Wandrei

Hello! My name is Angel Dog Austin
and I live in doggy heaven.
It's not the same as people heaven,
but it's perfect for us dogs.

A dog's life on earth can be a truly interesting thing to read about, but life up here...well, **"AMAZING"** isn't even a big enough word!

Not only are the clouds my pillows and the streets lined
with treat bones, but the colors are much more brilliant and
magnificent. If doggy heaven is this great, can you
imagine what people heaven must be like?
wow!

And there is music – beautiful, magical music. So perfect and so clear.

I get to talk with God anytime I want
and I have learned so much.

Did you know that **dog** is **God** spelled backwards?

God told me that we dogs are made
very much like His love...

patient...

Dogs can remind you of God's love in many ways.
We don't need to use words to be
heard or understood...

we love to hear praise...

And when you are sad or lonely, we curl up right next to you until you feel better and to remind you that you are not alone.

God also told me that there are rooms in people heaven just bursting
at the seams with gifts He has waiting for people who just need to ask
for them. Not the kind of presents you get for your birthday,
but presents for your heart. God showed me the rooms,
and He is not kidding – the iron gates are bending
and the hinges are ready to **Snap!**

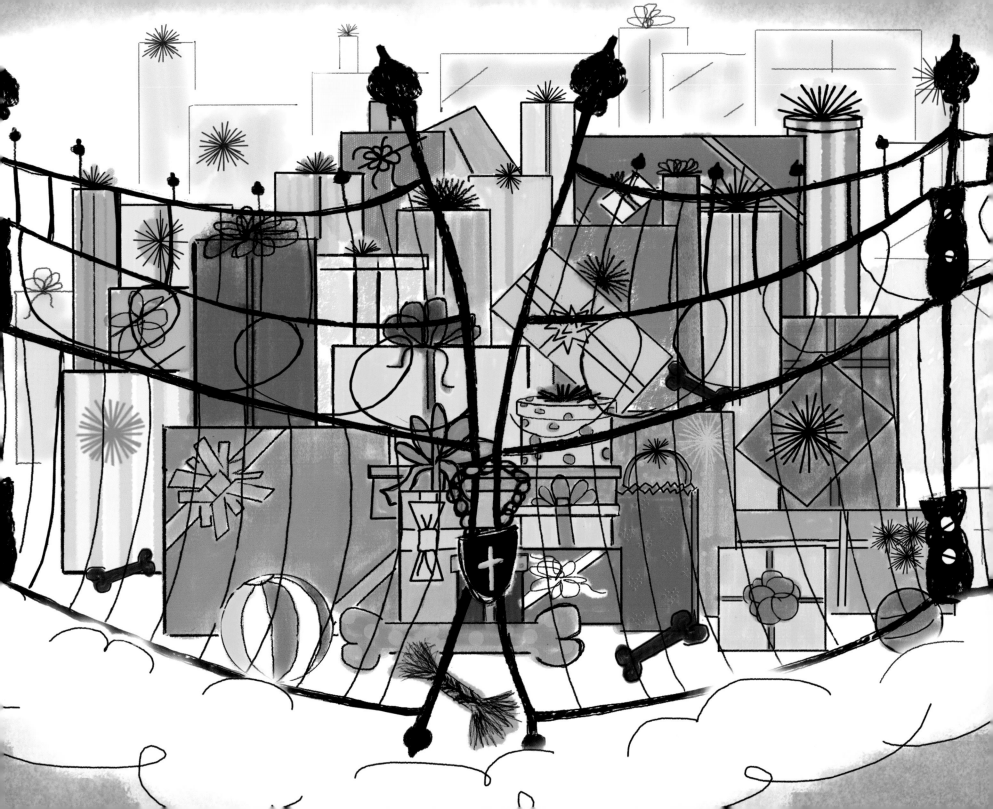

Of course, the greatest gift God has
ever given to us is His son, Jesus.
He is a gift to be loved.

ALL you need to do is accept God's gift
and invite Jesus into your heart.

It doesn't matter if you've been
really, really good...

...or if you've been a little naughty.

Once you accept Jesus into your heart to love you just the way you are, those iron gates holding back all the presents burst open sending gifts of love out and down through the clouds.

Some of the presents land by me and I give them a shove off my cloud so no one will miss any hope, or a kiss, or a hug, or a smile, or a blessing, or a friend, or anything they have needed for so long. And, the gift always fits perfectly for the special person who receives it.

Well, I could go on and on about all the wonderful, amazing things up here. But just remember, if you have ever loved and been loved by a dog, you have a glimpse of what it is like to be loved by God. Of course, your dog's capacity to love you doesn't come close to how much God loves you, but they both feel

mighty good!

God loves you!

John 3:16

"For God so loved the world that He gave His one and only Son, that whoever believes in Him shall not perish, but have eternal life."